A Firefly Book

Published under license by Firefly Books Ltd. 2017

Adapted from the animated short film *The Cat Came Back*

First printing

Publisher Cataloging-in-Publication Data (U.S.)
Names: Barker, Cordell, author.
Title: The Cat Came Back / Cordell Barker.
Description: Richmond Hill, Ontario, Canada : Firefly Books, 2017. | Summary: This book is based on a short animated film that was based on the traditional children's song.
Identifiers: ISBN 978-1-77085-929-6 (hardcover)
Subjects: LCSH: Cats -- Juvenile fiction. | Stories in rhyme. | BISAC: JUVENILE FICTION / Animals / Cats. | JUVENILE FICTION / Media Tie-In.
Classification: LCC PZ7.B354Ca |DDC [E] – dc23

Library and Archives Canada Cataloguing in Publication
A CIP record for this title is available from Library and Archives Canada

Published in the United States by
Firefly Books (U.S.) Inc.
P.O. Box 1338, Ellicott Station
Buffalo, New York 14205

Published in Canada by
Firefly Books Ltd.
50 Staples Avenue, Unit 1
Richmond Hill, Ontario L4B 0A7

Cover and interior design: Barb Kelly

Printed in China

Canada We acknowledge the financial support of the Government of Canada.

The NFB is Canada's public producer of award-winning creative documentaries, auteur animation, and groundbreaking interactive stories, installations and participatory experiences. NFB producers are deeply embedded in communities across the country, working with talented artists and creators in production studios from St. John's to Vancouver, on projects that stand out for their excellence in storytelling, their innovation, and their social resonance. NFB productions have won over 5,000 awards, including 15 Canadian Screen Awards, 17 Webbys, 12 Oscars® and more than 90 Genies. To access many of these works, visit NFB.ca or download the NFB's apps for mobile devices and connected TV.

The three things he loved more than anything else were

1. His old baby rattle

2. His mother

3. His tuba.

He was also very fond of his one remaining hair.

MOM

1903

BRUMP!
BRUMPFT!

BRUMP!
BRUMPFT!
BRUMP!

He spent most of his time blowing into his tuba. This really rattled the windows.

Who could be banging
at his door so loudly?

It's a cat!

Normally, Old Mr. Johnson would have shooed that little yellow cat away. But ...

... this little yellow cat *WAS* kind of cute. And Old Mr. Johnson *WAS* kind of lonely. Playing with this little yellow cat would be lots of fun!

Oh no! That rattle was his favorite thing in the whole world!

Mr. Johnson didn't want to play any more. So, he decided to take the little yellow cat for a nice drive and ...

... lose him in the woods!

CRACK!

AAAGH!

The only one who got lost in the woods was Old Mr. Johnson! It would be a long walk home to his empty house.

How did the little yellow cat make it all the way back to his house?

Old Mr. Johnson needed a better plan to get rid of this little yellow pest. He would ...

... strand the cat at sea!

SPLOOSH!

The only one who went
for a swim was Old Mr. Johnson!

ZOOM!

BUT the cat came back the very next day.

Unbelievable! Didn't the little yellow cat get it? Old Mr. Johnson wanted him gone. G-O-N-E!

Next he'd try a different direction ...

... and fly the cat up, up and away!

He had a good plan. But Old Mr. Johnson learned the hard way that what goes up ...

... must come down!

The little yellow cat was back! He'd ruined everything! Old Mr. Johnson was beginning to lose his mind.

Next he'd make sure the cat couldn't squirm free. He would ...

... tie the little yellow cat to the tracks!

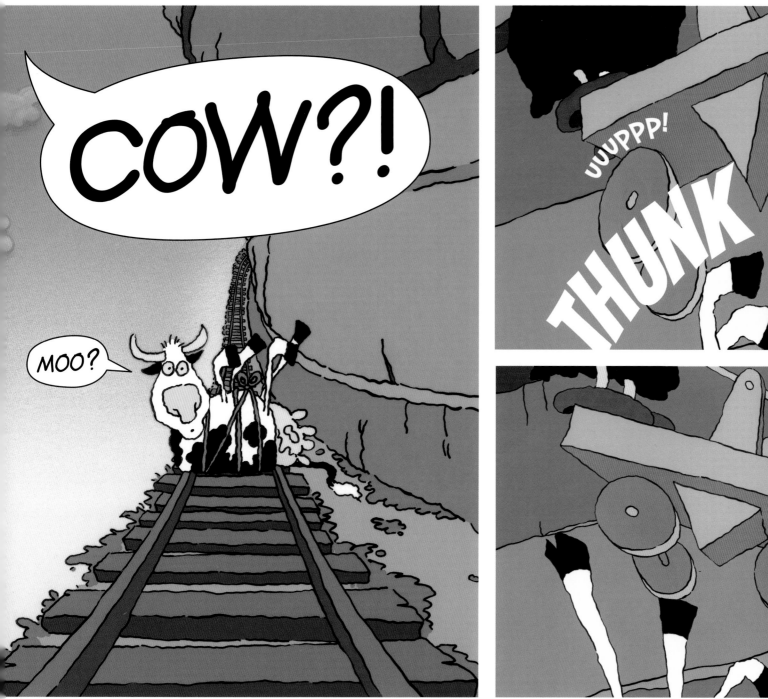

... but they jumped over the cow!

... Old Mr. Johnson was sent tumbling down by the teeny, tiniest green beetle.

Old Mr. Johnson hit rock bottom.

Old Mr. Johnson suddenly had a *BIG* idea! The little yellow cat couldn't come back if there was no house to come back to.

MUAHAHA!

He would blow up his house!

With this much dynamite there was no way the cat could ever come back!

BUT instead of lighting the dynamite fuse, he lit his last precious hair!

Hooray! Old Mr. Johnson had finally gotten rid of the little yellow cat for good! But ...

... he forgot that cats have *NINE* lives!

Now, *NINE* little yellow cats would keep coming back forever!

Old Mr. Johnson thought the cat was a goner ...

... but he just wouldn't stay away.